CONTENTS

KU-443-497

LIBRARIES NI
WITHDRAWN FROM STOCK

CHAPTER 1

Something Strange

Pete Brundle and his best friend Krish were looking at their phones in the dinner hall, ignoring the commotion around them. They weren't supposed to use phones at school, but there was another weird story on their favourite website, The Mystery Shed. The story was about a town in Australia that had been over-run by spiders. There was even a video, so it was too good to miss.

"That's awesome," Pete said. "I wish something like that would happen in Crooked Oak. This village is so boring. Nothing ever—"

BAM!

Someone slammed into them, and Krish's new phone went flying. It hit the floor with a *CRACK!* and spun under the nearest table.

Krish dropped down and scooted after it. Pete turned to see their friend Nancy Finney standing behind him. She was the smartest kid in Year Eight. Short and skinny with hair the colour of autumn leaves, Nancy had pale blue eyes and a spattering of freckles on her cheeks.

"What did you do that for?" Pete said, frowning.

"Sorry," Nancy said. "That big idiot pushed me."

"Who are you calling an idiot?" Tyson Bridges said. He was in the year above them and twice as big as everyone else in school.

"I'm calling *you* an idiot," Nancy said, looking up at him. "Why don't you watch where you're going?"

Tyson balled his meaty hands into fists. "You're that kid whose mum works at the fracking site, aren't you?" he said. "On Carpenter's Field. It's out of bounds now, and we can't play there any more. My dad says your mum's a traitor for working there and that everyone in the village hates her."

"Leave Nancy alone," Pete told Tyson, and stood up. "The fracking site has been closed down now, haven't you heard? And you *do* know her dad's the Head Teacher?"

"So?" Tyson glared at Pete. "One more reason to hate her."

"Well ..." Pete tilted his head. "He's right over there."

Tyson narrowed his eyes at Mr Finney standing by the dinner-hall entrance. Tyson's hands relaxed and he leaned close to Nancy as he said, "I'll be watching you."

Tyson stalked away, and Nancy went to collect her dinner.

"Thanks for sticking up for me," she said as she came back to the table and sat down on the opposite bench.

"No problemo," Pete replied. He brushed a strand of blond hair away from his forehead, then shovelled half a roast potato into his mouth.

Krish was checking his phone, muttering that his mum would kill him if it was broken.

"Do you guys want to hear something really weird?" Nancy said.

"Like what?" Krish asked, and glanced up at her.

Nancy sighed and put her hand to her mouth as if she didn't want to say it. "It's my mum and dad," she began. "I mean ... there's something strange about them."

"Strange?" Krish pushed his glasses up his nose, making his dark brown eyes look enormous. This was his serious mode.

"Yeah, they've changed," Nancy went on. "It's like they're not really my parents."

"In what way?" Krish asked, looking interested.

"Well, you know when someone's mouth smiles but their eyes don't? They're like that. No emotion." Nancy stared at the lunch congealing on her plate. "This probably sounds stupid, but when I told Mum I got an A in my Maths test yesterday, she hardly said a word. Normally she makes a big fuss."

"Is that it?" Krish asked. He sounded unimpressed, and Pete knew why. Krish got a B in that test, and he hated being the *second* smartest kid in their class. His mum and dad expected him to be top in everything, no excuses. Krish said he had a "Tiger Mum, Indian Style", and he was right – Pete had met her.

"No, that's not it," Nancy said. "Mum and Dad have started keeping the curtains closed all the time, even when it's sunny outside. And they keep going out at strange times during the night."

"Doesn't sound *that* weird," Krish said. "My mum keeps the blinds closed all day. She says it stops the photos on the wall from fading."

Pete nudged Krish to shut up, then gave Nancy a supportive look. "When did it start?" Pete asked her.

Nancy thought for a moment. "A few days ago, maybe? Not long after the fracking site was shut down." Her face lit up as if she'd suddenly remembered something. "Yeah," Nancy added. "Dad took Mum down there to pick up some files, and they were acting weird when they got back."

Their Geography teacher had given them a lesson about Hydraulic Fracturing, or "fracking" as everyone was calling it, when the site at Carpenter's Field had first opened. Mr Craven had explained how the people from the gas company would drill into the ground, pump in water, sand and chemicals, then suck it all back out again. That would release gas to power central heating systems and cookers and other things.

But everyone in the village had been furious about the idea. They'd said fracking could cause small earthquakes. They'd also said that the chemicals used were highly poisonous and could get into the drinking water. It had been all anyone in Crooked Oak had talked about for months. Loads of protests had taken place outside Carpenter's Field. People with banners, shouting and getting angry.

Pete wasn't listening to Nancy any more. He was thinking about how he and Krish and Nancy used to spend time building camps in the woods around Carpenter's Field – before it'd been fenced off. But now that the fracking site had suddenly been shut down, Pete wondered if they'd get the field back soon. No one really seemed to know what was going on with it.

"I used to love playing in Carpenter's Field," Pete said. "Remember how we used to catch those tiny fish in the beck?"

"Sticklebacks," Nancy said. "I remember. And my mum wasn't doing the drilling – she just worked at the fracking site because she needed a job. She was in the *office*. And anyway—"

"It's all right," Pete said. "We know it's not your fault."

"I wish everyone else did," Nancy said as she pushed a piece of soggy broccoli around her

plate. "People like Tyson Bridges keep saying my mum's a traitor."

"Ignore them," Pete told her.

They sat in silence for a while, picking at their food, until Nancy said, "So what do you think? About my mum and dad?"

Krish shrugged. "Doesn't sound that weird to me."

But Pete wasn't so sure. He'd always liked Mr Finney, but when Pete looked back now and saw the Head Teacher staring right at them, he couldn't help feeling creeped out.

There was a strange, dead look in Mr Finney's eyes.

CHAPTER 2

Carpenter's Field

At the end of school, Pete and Krish went to get their bikes, while Nancy went to her music lesson.

"I reckon Nancy's mum and dad are vampires," Pete said to Krish. "They went down to the fracking place to get some files and got bitten."

Krish rolled his eyes. "You're obsessed with vampires! You need to read more instead of playing video games and watching horror films all the time."

"But it makes sense," Pete insisted. "They keep the curtains closed, so they must be scared of daylight. And they keep going out at night."

"They're not vampires, Pete," Krish said.

They unlocked their bikes and wheeled them to the school gates.

"Do you have to get home straight away?" Pete asked.

"Why?" Krish asked.

"Come with me."

Pete and Krish pedalled out of school, through the village and along Ridley Lane. The wind was cold on their faces as they rode between the high hedges on each side of the lane.

"We're going to Carpenter's Field?" Krish asked as he worked hard to keep up with Pete. "What for?"

"I just want to have a look," Pete said.

When they reached Carpenter's Field, the boys stopped. The enormous field was surrounded by a tall hedge and there were woods in the distance. Crows flew in circles above the golden treetops, cawing in the afternoon autumn air.

The field had been a special place as long as Pete could remember. Generations of kids from Crooked Oak had built camps here. Everyone used to come and play football, and hide and seek. They'd netted sticklebacks in the stream and swung over it on the old frayed rope.

But a few months ago, the gas company had put a chain-link fence around it all, double the height of the boys, topped with barbed wire. The only way in was through a locked gate. They had torn up the ground to build a well pad – a huge rectangle of concrete. And the site was filled with rows of enormous metal shipping containers and portable offices. Trucks had been coming and going along Ridley Lane for weeks.

Pete hadn't seen the fracking site since it was first built. He hadn't been able to go to the protests because Mum was having one of her chronic back-pain attacks. He spent most of his time looking after her when he wasn't at school.

"It looks different now," Pete said. "Something's changed."

"It's the drill tower," Krish said. "They came a couple of weeks ago and put that building round it. No one knows why."

In the middle of the site was a large metal building painted red. "BioMesa" was written across the side of it in big white letters. A tall drilling tower rose from the centre of it, like a complicated mesh of scaffolding.

"And now it's all closed down," Krish said.

"It's so quiet." Pete shuddered. "It's creepy." It was cold, and his breath came out in clouds.

A magpie suddenly chattered in the branches of a conker tree behind them, on the other side of the lane. Krish jumped and gave Pete a sheepish look.

"So if they're not vampires, what are they?" Pete asked, and felt a shiver of nervous excitement. "Nancy said her mum and dad started acting weird after they'd been here to collect papers or something. And why did they put in that new building, then close it all down? It's *definitely* a mystery."

"Is it?" Krish took a pack of gum from his pocket. "Do you remember that story on The Mystery Shed about the woman who thought her daughter was an imposter – a stranger pretending to be her daughter?"

"The one in America?" Pete said.

"Yeah. Turned out the woman had something called Capgras Syndrome. A condition that makes people think their family are imposters." Krish popped a piece of gum into his mouth and threw the pack to Pete. "So maybe Nancy has Capgras Syndrome."

Pete fumbled as he tried to catch the gum and it dropped into a puddle. "Sorry," he said, and pulled a face. "Wait. You think she's imagining it?"

"She could be," Krish said.

"But Nancy said her mum and dad keep all the curtains closed during the day. And they've got no emotions."

Krish shrugged. "That doesn't mean they're not her mum and dad. Or that they're vampires."

"OK, but maybe there's something else wrong with them," Pete said. "Come on, this is what we've always wanted. Crooked Oak is so boring, nothing ever happens, but now we've got a mystery. I mean, even if it's *not* a mystery, at least we can have fun investigating. Think about it."

"All right." Krish ran a hand through his black spiky hair. "I'll think about it. And you owe me some gum."

CHAPTER 3

Eyes of the Dead

When Pete arrived home, his mum was in the sitting room.

"Good day at school?" she asked.

"Uh-huh," Pete replied. "Your back still bad?"

"Oh, it'll get better." His mum struggled to her feet and limped into the kitchen. "It just takes a while."

It had always just been Pete and his mum at home. His dad died before Pete was old enough to remember him. There were photos of Dad on the windowsill in the living room, but the man in the pictures might as well have been a complete stranger.

"I'll get tea," Pete said. "You just sit down and rest your back." It made him sad to see his mum struggling so much.

Pete made beans on toast, and they ate it at the kitchen table.

"Thanks, love, you're such a gem." Mum managed half a piece of toast and a few forks of beans before she pushed the plate away. "I'm so sick of this pain. A group of villagers is touring the Carpenter's Field fracking site this evening. They're going to talk about what will happen now it's closed, and I really wanted to go but ..." Mum sighed. "I just don't think I can make it."

"I'm glad you're not going," Pete said. "That place is creepy."

After tea, Mum took her tablets and went to bed saying her back was too painful to sit and watch TV. Pete finished his homework in his bedroom, then fired up his clunky old laptop instead of playing video games.

Slumped in his beanbag, Pete looked up as much as he could about fracking, and anything he could find about Carpenter's Field. After that, he searched The Mystery Shed for something similar to Nancy's story. The only video Pete found was the one Krish had mentioned about Capgras Syndrome, but Nancy seemed so normal. So *sane*. Pete just couldn't bring himself to believe that Nancy was imagining it all.

*

Pete was up early the next day for his paper round. Mum couldn't work when her back was bad, so it was his way of earning some extra money to help out. Pete checked on her, made her a cup of tea, then biked to King's Corner Shop while stuffing down a piece of buttered toast. Mr King always cheered Pete up with his friendly smile and his corny joke of the day.

"Morning," Pete called as the bell jangled over the shop door.

Pete had been doing the paper round for Mr King for almost a year, and they knew each other well. Normally it was difficult to get Mr King to stop talking, but this morning he stood silently in the shadow behind the counter.

It was then that Pete realised how dark it was inside the shop. There weren't any lights on at all. And there was a strange but familiar musty smell.

"Umm," Pete said, remembering what Nancy had told him about her parents sitting in the dark. "Paper round?"

Instead of giving Pete his usual chirpy smile, Mr King pointed at the bag on the counter and said, "All there." His voice was lower than usual.

"Right." Pete walked up to the counter and caught sight of Mr King's eyes. They were blank. No expression at all. They were exactly how Pete imagined the eyes of the dead would be.

"How's your mum?" Mr King asked, but there was no emotion in his voice. It sounded like he didn't care one jot about Pete's mum.

"Um ... fine." Pete paused. "Are you ... all right, Mr King?"

"Couldn't be better," Mr King replied. His soft words were like cold fingers sliding down Pete's spine.

Pete snatched the satchel of newspapers, then backed away and made his escape into the fresh air.

He jumped on his bike and scanned the centre of the village as he rode away. There were two people getting into a car on the other side of the green, and a man walking his dog,

but it seemed quieter than usual. Pete began to ride around the village delivering newspapers and noticed that a lot of curtains were closed and there were fewer people in the streets heading to work. He had the feeling that something wasn't quite right about Crooked Oak.

Something felt different.

CHAPTER 4

Freaky Weird

"There's something going on," Pete said as soon as he sat down next to Krish in form time. "Mr King was acting weird this morning. Like *freaky weird*. And the village is really quiet. It creeped me out doing my paper round."

"Sure you're not just imagining it?" Krish asked. "After everything Nancy said yesterday, maybe you're—"

"Imagining it? No way," Pete said. "I'm telling you, Mr King was acting strange."

When Nancy came in and joined them, she looked pale and tired. And scared.

"What's the matter?" Pete asked. "Is it your mum and dad?"

Nancy nodded. "They're getting worse. I don't think I've seen them eat anything for at least two days. They drink water, but they don't eat, and they keep the curtains drawn so it's always dark. My dad's normally really stingy when it comes to putting the heating on, but now it's on full blast, so it's roasting. I'm walking about in a T-shirt, but they're wearing jumpers and coats!" Nancy stopped babbling and put her head in her hands. "I'm scared. Something's happened to them, and I don't know what to do."

Pete looked over at the open classroom door and saw that the lights were off in the corridor. Nancy's dad was out there, watching them from the shadows. His skin was pale, and there was a blank look in his eyes. He was wearing a thick overcoat, yet it was boiling in school.

"He's right there," Pete whispered without moving his lips.

Nancy didn't look up. "The worst thing is the smell," she said. "At first there was only a bit of it, but now ... it's disgusting. It's like when we had fungus growing in the bathroom in our old house."

"Fungus," Pete said as he suddenly remembered. "That's it. I smelled the same thing in Mr King's shop. I knew I recognised it. It's like those musty black splotches in the corners above the shower. Mum makes me spray everything after I've been in."

"Exactly like that," Nancy agreed. "But ten times worse. And it's not the house that smells, it's *them*. After Mum and Dad went out to give everyone that tour of Carpenter's Field last night, the house started to smell normal again."

"What?" Krish asked, looking up from his phone. He was searching The Mystery Shed again. "What tour?"

"Mum was showing people the fracking site," Nancy said. "Letting them look inside and talking about what's going to happen to it now they've stopped fracking."

"Yeah, my mum mentioned that," Pete chipped in. "She couldn't go because of her back."

Krish pushed up his glasses. "I heard Tracey Levin say her parents were acting weird this morning. Weren't they leading the protests? I'm sure they would've been on that tour."

Pete stared at Krish, shocked. "I bet Mr King was there too. I bet *all* the shopkeepers were. They all had those 'Keep Carpenter's Field Natural' signs in their windows."

"Maybe there's a connection," Krish said, and looked at Nancy. "You told us your mum and dad started acting weird after they went to Carpenter's Field to collect files, right?"

"Right."

"And after the tour last night, Tracey Levin's parents are acting weird." Krish tapped his fingers on the desk as he put it all together. "Mr King too."

"So now you believe me?" Nancy asked.

"I'm not saying that," Krish said. "But maybe we *should* investigate. We'll go to your house after school and see for ourselves what your mum and dad are like."

CHAPTER 5

A Stab of Fear

Mr Finney was at the gates when school ended, wearing his long coat with the hood pulled up, even though it was sunny. He was handing out letters and reminding everyone about an important "emergency" meeting in the school hall at seven o'clock that evening. Something to do with cracking down on the use of mobile phones in school.

He lifted a hand to wave at Nancy as she rode past with Pete and Krish. Pete looked back and saw Mr Finney watching them with a blank stare. The breeze ruffled the letters gripped firmly in his right hand.

On the way to Nancy's house, they rode past the parade of shops in the village centre. There was a sign in the window of Hutson's Hardware advertising Aqua-Zap water guns for half price. Typical – Pete had paid full price at the beginning of summer.

When they reached King's Corner Shop, Krish braked suddenly and jumped off his bike. "Just a minute. I've got an idea," he said as he ran into the shop, leaving Pete and Nancy waiting outside.

Krish came back out a few minutes later carrying a flat cardboard box about the size of a school exercise book. It had a metallic red lid.

"Was Mr King in there?" Pete asked. "Did he seem weird?"

"A bit," Krish said. "He didn't say much."

"What about his eyes?" Pete went on. "Did they look blank?"

"And was it dark in there?" Nancy added.

Krish shrugged. "Yeah, but maybe he had a headache or something."

"Ugh. Stop being so logical," Pete said. "And what's that for?" He pointed at the box in Krish's hands. The gold lettering across the top said "Turkish Delight".

"It's a test." Krish gave the box a shake and looked at Nancy. "I reckon your mum *loves* this stuff. I once saw her eat a whole box of it while she was having tea with my mum."

"I remember that," Nancy said. "And you're right, she really *does* love it. But so what?"

"You said your mum hasn't eaten anything for two days." Krish shook the box again. "Well, let's see if she refuses *this*."

"I still don't get it," Pete complained.

"Don't you see?" Nancy said to him. "If my mum refuses Turkish Delight, then there's *definitely* something wrong with her."

*

The first thing Pete noticed when Nancy opened her front door was the mouldy smell that spilled out into the crisp autumn evening. The second thing was the heat. It was as if she had opened an oven door.

Standing on the doorstep, Pete whispered in Krish's ear, "You sure about this?"

"Yes." Krish adjusted his glasses. "Of course."

Nancy's mum was normally bouncy and loud. She loved to talk and *always* met them with a big smile, but today she just stood in the darkness by the kitchen door at the end of the hall.

"Hello," she said in a low, monotonous voice as they draped their coats over the bannister. "How about some hot chocolate and biscuits?"

When Mrs Finney turned and went into the kitchen, Pete and Nancy hung back by the front door.

"Come on!" Krish hissed at them as he clutched the box of Turkish Delight and followed Mrs Finney.

It was dark and hot and smelled damp in the kitchen. The sun was still out, but the blinds were pulled over the windows.

Nancy's mum put the kettle on, then poured herself a glass of water from the tap. She drained it in a few swallows and left the empty glass beside the sink. "Your friends can't stay long – Dad will be home soon," Mrs Finney said without emotion. "And then we have to get ready to go out."

Nancy frowned.

"The meeting," her mum said. "Seven o'clock at school. It's very important."

Krish was watching Nancy's mum so closely that Pete had to nudge him forward with the Turkish Delight.

Krish held it out. "For you, Mrs Finney. It's your favourite, right?"

With a waft of damp, mouldy smell, Nancy's mum came forward to take it. As she did, she stepped into a beam of sunlight that had found a crack in the blinds. It cut across the gloomy kitchen like a glowing sword. When it touched the skin on Mrs Finney's hand, she jumped back as if she'd had an electric shock.

Krish gasped in surprise.

And in that split-second, Pete saw that Mrs Finney's eyes were so bloodshot that the whites were almost red.

"Are you all right, Mum?" Nancy asked.

"Fine." Mrs Finney put her hand behind her back and forced an empty smile at Krish. "Why don't you put that on the table?"

Krish hesitated, and Pete saw that all the colour had drained from his friend's face. Krish was finally starting to believe that something strange was going on. How could he *not* believe it?

Pete took the box and stepped forward, trying not to gag on the smell. "I could open it for you?" he said to Mrs Finney. "You could try some now."

"No. Thank you."

"It's from Krish's mum," Pete added. His hands were trembling. "She'll want to know if you liked it, so ..." He tore the wrapper off and opened the box. Each chunk of hard jelly was dusted with half a ton of icing sugar. "You'd better try it or she'll give Krish grief."

"All right," Mrs Finney gave in. "Just a small piece."

Pete watched closely as she bit into it and chewed.

"Delicious." Mrs Finney went to the sink and poured herself another glass of water.

Pete couldn't help feeling a bit disappointed. Mrs Finney had passed Krish's test. But that didn't make her normal. What about her voice? And her eyes? And that smell?

And there was something else: Pete put the box of Turkish Delight on the worktop and saw a half-chewed chunk of it lying in the sink. He felt a stab of fear and excitement. Mrs Finney *hadn't* eaten it. She'd spat it out when she was pouring another glass of water.

"Well, it was nice to see you, Mrs Finney," Pete said. He grabbed Krish's arm and made sure he saw what was in the sink. "But we have to go now. Come on, Nancy, we have that thing, remember?"

"What thing?" Nancy was confused for a moment, then her eyes widened as she understood. "Oh. That thing. OK. We'd better go."

The three of them bustled from the kitchen and snatched their coats from the bannister. At that moment, the front door swung open to reveal Mr Finney standing on the doorstep.

His empty eyes stared down at them from beneath his hood.

"In a hurry?" Mr Finney asked.

"We have a thing, sir," Pete said. "We need to go."

Mr Finney ignored him and looked at Nancy. "Where are you off to?" he asked her, and blocked the doorway. "Don't forget the meeting. Everyone must be there. Your parents too." Mr Finney stared at Pete and Krish.

"Mum can't make it," Pete said. "Bad back again. Can't sit down for more than a few minutes."

Mr Finney opened his mouth to say something, but Nancy pushed past and the boys hurried after her.

"Everyone must be there!" Mr Finney called after them. "It's important!"

*

Nancy, Krish and Pete rode away as fast as they could, but at the corner at the end of the street, Nancy screeched to a halt. "See," she said. "There's something wrong with them. I told you."

"We believe you," Pete replied, and looked at Krish. "Don't we?"

"Did you see her eyes?" Krish said. "What was wrong with her eyes?"

CHAPTER 6

In the Shadows

"I'm not going back home," Nancy said. She wiped her eyes and gave Pete and Krish a pleading look. "Don't leave me on my own."

"We won't," Pete told her.

"And you'll help me?" Nancy asked.

"Of course." Pete turned to Krish and lowered his voice. "How do we help her?"

"Umm." Krish shook himself. "I'm not sure. Maybe we could—"

A loud rattling sound shattered the quiet evening, making them all turn to look along Elm Street, towards Nancy's house.

"That's our garage door," Nancy said. "It always rattles like that."

It was just starting to get dark, but they could see Nancy's garage door roll up. A moment later, Nancy's mum and dad drove out in a red van. There was a white logo painted on the side of the van:

BioMesa.

"Where are they going?" Nancy wondered out loud. "What time is it?"

"It's just after five o'clock," Krish said, checking his phone. "They're too early for the meeting at school."

As the garage door clattered shut, the van pulled off the drive and headed in the opposite direction along Elm Street.

"Come on." Pete jumped on his bike. "Let's see where they're going."

*

They followed the red van along Elm Street, then into the heart of the village and out the other side onto Ridley Lane.

"They're going to Carpenter's Field," Krish said.

When the van stopped at the gates, the headlights lit up the main building with BioMesa painted across the side.

Nancy's dad stepped out of the van and went to unlock and open the gates. The evening was fresh and clear, and already a bright sliver of moon was sitting among the stars.

"I was reading about fracking last night," Pete whispered. "About all those chemicals they pump into the ground to get the gas out. It's all poisonous stuff, you know. Maybe it did something to them. Turned them into freaks."

A vehicle door slammed and they turned their attention back to the van. It was now driving into the Carpenter's Field fracking site.

As soon as the van was inside, Pete, Nancy and Krish followed. They put their phones on silent and wheeled their bikes behind the shipping containers. Hiding in the shadows, they watched Nancy's mum and dad climb out of the van and disappear inside the main building.

"Should we follow them?" Nancy said, standing up.

"No way." Krish grabbed the back of her coat. "Stay where you are."

"But we don't know what they're doing in there." Nancy pulled away from Krish.

As she stepped forward, the door opened and Nancy's mum reappeared. She was carrying a crate of shoebox-sized packages which she slid into the back of the van.

A moment later, Nancy's dad appeared, carrying another crate.

"What's in those boxes?" Krish wondered aloud.

Nancy's mum and dad made several trips, filling the van with boxes, then climbed into the cab. They turned the vehicle around to head back to the gates, and Nancy grabbed her bike, ready to follow them.

"Let them go," Krish said, stopping her. "We should investigate that building."

CHAPTER 7

A Terrible Discovery

To Pete's surprise, the door to the BioMesa building was unlocked. He pulled it open and sneaked in first. "It's so hot in here," Pete said as he felt the wall, searching for a light switch. When he found one, he flicked it, expecting the place to light up like a Christmas tree, but nothing happened.

"No power." Pete remembered how Mrs Finney had reacted to the beam of sunlight in her kitchen. "Or they took out the lightbulbs."

"It stinks," Krish said, following Pete inside. "I've changed my mind. I don't like this." He turned to leave, but Nancy held on to him.

"We need to stick together," she said.

They took out their phones and switched on the torches, but the huge room was *so* dark it swallowed the light. Everything was black, black, black.

The deeper they went, the stronger the mouldy smell became. "The ground feels funny," Nancy said. She shone the torch at her feet. "It's spongy." She crouched, bringing the torchlight closer to the floor. Twists of fine fibres formed a miniature landscape of hills and forests covering the ground. When Nancy shifted her feet, the awful mouldy smell wafted up at them.

"It's some kind of fungus." Nancy put out her hand.

"Don't touch it," Krish said. "Don't touch anything. We should tell someone about this."

"In a minute." Pete shone his torch ahead. "I think I see something."

In the centre of the building was the lower section of the drilling rig. It looked like tall scaffolding over the roof outside, but inside it was totally different. Huge black vines snaked around it, forming a smooth, shining black trunk. They twisted up to the ceiling and spread out like branches. When Pete directed his torch at them, the vines shrank away from the light.

"We should leave," Krish said. "I don't want to investigate this any more."

Nancy shone her torch at a huge hole beneath the rig, where the black fungus had erupted in vines from the earth. "Maybe the fracking disturbed it," Nancy said. "Released it from underground, I mean."

"Keep away," Krish said in a low, scared voice.

"What about the people who came on the tour last night?" Nancy said. "If they came in here, they must have seen this. The way they're acting, and the way my mum and dad are acting ... It's got to be connected to this."

Pete moved closer to the main stem of the giant fungus. The ground squished and squelched with every step. "You've got to see this," he said.

Hundreds of bent limbs burst out from the spongy trunk. At the end of each limb was something that looked like a claw. Most of the claws were empty, but one or two gripped pods the size of grapefruits. They were deep purple and covered with thousands of tiny white spots.

"They look like spore pods," Krish whispered. "Like you find on a fungus, but bigger."

"So what were my mum and dad doing in here just now?" Nancy said.

"This might be a clue." Pete called them over to a long table that was piled with boxes.

"Those are the boxes Mum and Dad were putting in the van," Nancy said. She lifted one of the lids. "And there's one of those pod things in it."

When they peered in to look at it, the purple pod began to beat like a heart.

"Get back!" Pete shouted. He slammed the lid shut and pulled Nancy away. "I've seen *Alien* – I know what happens next. That thing bursts and ..." He spread his fingers wide and clamped them over his face. "Argh!"

"Stop messing about," Krish said, pushing up his glasses and giving Pete a serious look. "It's not funny."

"And I'm not joking," Pete said. "It wasn't supposed to be funny."

Nancy hugged both arms around herself. "Where do you think Mum and Dad were taking these thi—" She turned to Pete and Krish with a look of horror. "The 'emergency' meeting," she said.

"What?" Pete was confused.

"The meeting at school," Krish reminded him. "Everyone's supposed to be there." Krish started tapping on his phone. "Maybe it's nothing to do with cracking down on mobile phones like the letter said. Maybe they're going to do something with these *things*. We have to tell someone. I'll call my parents and ... oh my days." Krish stopped. "No signal."

Nancy checked her phone. "Same here."

"We'll go to my house," Krish said, and started towards the front door. "It's closest. And I'm pretty sure my mum and dad are still normal."

"There's no point," Nancy told Krish, going after him. "Look at the time. We've been here longer than we thought, and the school meeting's about to start. Your mum and dad will be there already. They've probably been trying to ring you."

"You're right." Krish paused with his hand on the door handle and looked back at Nancy. "We should go straight to school."

"So you don't think we're imagining it any more?" Pete asked.

"No," Krish replied. He pushed open the door and hurried outside.

"But other people might think we are," Nancy said. "I'll take a picture to prove we're not." She pointed her camera upwards and took a photo. In the brief flash of bright white light, they all saw the roof of the building. It was covered with more of the bent claws holding pods. There were hundreds of them.

Maybe even thousands.

CHAPTER 8

Too Late

The cold wind bit at Nancy, Pete and Krish as they sped along Ridley Lane and headed back into the village. None of them spoke. Each was lost in thought about what they had seen at Carpenter's Field.

When they reached the school, the car park was full.

"Everyone's already here," Pete said as he skidded to a halt. "It must be most of the school."

"Still no signal," Krish said, holding his phone higher and frowning at the screen.

"Look." Nancy pointed. "That's my mum's van."

Pete rode over and pressed his face close to the van's back window. "The boxes are gone," he said.

"Come on." Krish dumped his bike and ran to the front of the school. "I see my parents' car. They must be inside."

But the main door was locked, so they raced around the school, looking into the dark windows and checking all the doors.

The fire escape at the side of the hall was sealed tight. When they put their ears to the painted wood, they heard the hubbub of a crowd.

"Everyone's in there," Krish said. He was starting to panic. "I bet those boxes are in there too. Those *things*."

Pete remembered the freaky pod, beating like a living heart.

"Open up!" Krish hammered on the door. "Open up!"

"They can't hear you," Nancy told him. "It's too noisy in there."

"I have to get in." Krish was growing more agitated. "My mum and dad are inside!"

Nancy stepped back and looked up at the narrow windows along the top of the hall. "If only we could see in."

"Maybe we can," Pete said. He led the others around the back of the hall and used the lower branches of an oak tree to climb onto the roof of the temporary history classroom.

From there, they had a perfect view into the high windows of the hall. They saw parents and kids chatting in the semi-darkness, waiting for the meeting to start. Even Tyson Bridges was there with his mum and dad.

"The boxes." Nancy's voice was so full of fear, it was like spiders crawling over Pete's skin. "Look."

Every single person had an unopened box on their lap.

"There's my mum and dad!" Krish pointed to a dark-haired couple sitting in the front row. There was an empty seat beside them, with a box ready for Krish. "I have to do something." He hurried along the roof and scrambled back down the tree.

Pete and Nancy didn't take their eyes off the windows. In the hall, Mr Finney had come onto the stage and was saying something to the audience.

Krish jumped to the ground with a thud and rushed around the side of the building. A few moments later, there was a loud banging.

"Mum! Dad!" Krish shouted, his voice cutting into the night.

In the hall, a few heads turned towards the fire-escape door, but Mr Finney continued talking. He had one of the boxes in his hand and was opening the lid. Pete guessed he was giving the audience instructions, because some of them were doing the same.

"Get out of there!" Krish's voice grew louder and shriller.

More heads turned towards the door, but already some of the parents at the other side of the hall had opened their boxes.

"It's too late," Nancy whispered.

Pete watched with dread as Krish's dad looked down into his box and—

POP!

Krish's dad's head jerked back as the pod burst and a musty cloud of spores erupted from the box.

A moment later, another parent opened their box. Then another. And with each explosion, the hall flooded with spores. Within seconds, there was a mist of particles floating over the audience's heads. Panicked parents and children were jerking and flinching in their seats. Some managed to get to their feet and make it to the doors, but they could only rattle on the handles, unable to get out.

Everything was locked. There was no way out of the hall.

Pete and Nancy watched the pandemonium. They couldn't look away. But soon the parents began to grow calm as the spores took effect. The first of the parents came to a standstill and turned like zombies towards the stage to look at Mr Finney, and Pete knew it was time to go.

*

Krish was still banging at the door when Pete grabbed him.

"My house!" Pete said. "My mum's not at the meeting. She'll know what to do."

"I can't leave them." Krish was frantic. His voice was hoarse from shouting.

"You have to," Pete told his friend. "It's not safe here. Everyone in there …" Pete looked at Nancy and saw the mix of fear and sadness in her eyes. "It's too late for them."

CHAPTER 9

Ambush

Campbell Street, where Pete lived, was eerily silent. No cars were on the move. No street lamps were glowing. No light spilled from closed curtains.

"I don't like it," Pete said as he stopped outside his house and looked around.

"I don't like *any* of this," Nancy said.

"Tell me again what you saw at school." Krish took off his glasses. He pinched the bridge of his nose and took a deep breath to calm himself. "Tell me *exactly*."

"We already told you a hundred times," Pete said, but he was glad to see his friend was in thinking mode now. Thinking Krish was more useful than panicking Krish.

"Basically, the spores came out and turned everyone into zombies," Nancy said. "Well, not zombies exactly, because zombies are dead, aren't they?"

"But it was definitely the spores?" Krish asked.

"Yes."

"So maybe it's like the ant-fungus we saw on The Mystery Shed," Krish said, looking at Pete. "The one that takes over ants' brains and makes them climb to the top of a tree."

"Why does it do that?" Nancy asked, sounding scared.

"Don't know," Krish said. He was lying and Pete knew why.

He knew which story Krish was talking about. Pete had loved it because there was a disgusting video to go with it, and Krish had hated it for the same reason. When the fungus-infected ants reached the tree tops, they died and exploded, sending spores across the jungle to infect more ants. The only purpose of the fungus was to survive and spread.

But the last thing any of them needed to think about was their parents' heads exploding.

"I need to check on my mum," Pete said. He abandoned his bike and hurried to the front door. His key clicked in the lock and the door eased open without a sound.

"Mum?" Pete hardly said it loud enough for Nancy and Krish to hear, let alone anyone in the house. "Mum? Are you here?" Pete went to the foot of the stairs and looked up into the darkness.

"Do you want me to go first?" Nancy asked.

Pete shook his head and started to climb the staircase. The others were close behind.

When they reached the top, Pete smelled the musty odour. His insides turned to water, and he wanted to get out. But the door at the end of the landing creaked open.

"Peter?" a voice said. "Is that you?"

Pete's mum was just a dark shape in the doorway. Moonlight spilled through the window behind her and cut across the landing carpet. His mum's long hair hung over her shoulders, shining with a silvery hue.

"Mum? Are you all right?" Pete asked.

"Peter. I have something for you." The ghostly figure held something out towards the children. Even in the darkness, they knew it was one of the strange purplish pods.

With panic flooding his veins, Pete started to back away. "She's infected!" he gasped.

Krish started downstairs, but when Pete turned to do the same, he saw another shape standing in the hallway below.

It was Nancy's mum. She came forward into the moonlight and raised her hands. "Nancy, darling," she said, and put her foot on the first step. "I have something for you."

And Pete realised it was his fault. He had told Mr Finney that his mum wouldn't be at the meeting. That was why Mrs Finney had come here – to make sure Pete's mum was infected like everyone else.

"No!" Pete cried. Guilt and fear washed over him as he looked from his mum to Nancy's mum. Both of them infected. Both of them carrying pods. Both of them moving closer.

"In here!" Nancy grabbed Pete's coat and dragged him towards the nearest door.

But it was too late for Krish. He turned to follow Pete and Nancy, but he was already halfway down the stairs—

POP!

A cloud of spores squirted from the pod in Mrs Finney's hands and shimmered in the moonlight. As Pete stumbled backwards into the bathroom, he saw a silvery mist envelop Krish. He stood bolt upright as if he'd been struck by lightning, and his fingers tightened on the bannister. Krish's eyes widened, and he stretched his mouth open as if he were about to scream and then—

SLAM!

Nancy pulled the bathroom door shut and pushed the bolt across.

CHAPTER 10

Escape

Nancy went straight to the window and threw it open. Cold, damp night air blew into the bathroom as she looked out. "It's too high," Nancy said. "We can't get out this way."

Beside her, Pete couldn't stop staring at the door.

"There must be something we can do," Nancy went on. "I don't want to be a mould monster. I don't want ... wait." She looked at Pete. "You said you had mould in the bathroom – that your mum makes you spray it."

"Yeah, with Mould Blaster but—"

"Where is it?" Nancy demanded.

"What?"

"The Mould Blaster!" yelled Nancy. *"Just get it!"*

Pete opened the cupboard under the sink and pulled out a spray bottle. He gave it a shake to test if it was full. "What now?" he asked.

"The black stuff you get in the bathroom is mould," Nancy said. "Which is a kind of fungus, so maybe the spray will kill the stuff that comes out of those pods. Maybe it'll stop our mums and Krish." Nancy pulled out her phone. "And we know they don't like bright light." She switched on the torch and went to the door. "Are you ready?"

Pete pointed the spray bottle at the door and took a deep breath. "OK," he said.

Nancy slid the bolt across and tugged the door wide.

Nancy's mum, Pete's mum and Krish reeled back at once from the torchlight, raising their arms to cover their eyes. Pete didn't waste time. He fired the spray, covering them in Mould Blaster. Immediately, they began to howl. It was the most awful sound Pete had ever heard – as if a thousand vampires were screaming at once.

And from somewhere outside came an ugly screaming reply.

SCREEEEEEEE!

Pete sprayed them again, and Krish collapsed. A moment later, Pete's mum and Nancy's mum followed suit, crashing to the carpet.

Nancy knelt beside her mum and felt her pulse with shaking hands. "She's still alive." She checked the others. "They're all still alive."

Pete looked at the spray bottle. "It worked," he said.

"But did you hear it?" Nancy asked. "When they made that awful noise, there was more screaming from outside."

Pete nodded. "There must be other Infected out there."

As if to confirm it, there was a rattle on the front door. Pete and Nancy hurried to the front bedroom and looked out of the window to see that Campbell Street was no longer deserted. There were now at least twenty Infected on the pavement below. Tyson Bridges was among them, staring up with blank eyes.

"They've come from school," Pete said. "How did they know we're here?"

"And how do we fight all of *them* with just a phone torch and a bottle of Mould Blaster?" Nancy asked.

Pete shrugged. "Don't know. But we have to try."

*

Pete and Nancy burst out of the front door, ready to fight. The first of the Infected to come at them was Tyson Bridges. He was slow and strong, striding down the path with the others following.

"Never liked you," Pete said as he gave Tyson two squirts of Mould Blaster.

Tyson let out a blood-freezing scream and stumbled backwards. Behind him, the others suddenly came to a stop and opened their mouths wide. They screamed together: a hideous chorus of screeching. Pete gave Tyson another blast, and the bully collapsed onto the concrete path. The other Infected staggered back, shocked and confused. Pete and Nancy took the chance to jump on their bikes and escape.

They rode fast, staying in the darkest shadows, finally slowing down as they travelled side by side past the park.

"Did you see that?" Pete asked, feeling the adrenaline pumping in his veins. "I sprayed Tyson Bridges." He couldn't help himself from grinning.

"I saw," Nancy replied, out of breath. "But did *you* see what happened to the others when you did it?"

Pete thought about all the screaming and blundering about. "Yeah. Why?"

"Same thing happened when you sprayed my mum." Nancy's nose was red with the cold.

"And my mum," Pete added. Suddenly it felt serious again. "And Krish."

"It affected them all, like they're connected somehow," Nancy said.

"So?"

"So, I mean, what if they *are* connected? What if they're part of the same thing? And what if that thing we saw at the fracking site is controlling them all?"

"Like a giant brain?" Pete suggested.

"Exactly," Nancy said. "So maybe we have to kill it. Kill the brain."

"With what? One bottle of Mould Blaster?"

"I think we'll need more than that. I have an idea."

*

They reached the village centre and went straight to Hutson's Hardware. Nancy snatched up one of the white-painted rocks that lined the green on the other side of the road.

"Sorry, Mr Hutson," she said just before she hefted the rock at the main window.

Immediately, they heard the shrill *SCREEEEEEEE* of the Infected. Pete looked across to see Mr Hutson standing on the green. He was wearing a thick winter coat and woolly hat. His mouth was open wide, and he was pointing a finger in their direction.

From somewhere in the village, a scream rang out in reply.

"Keep watch!" Nancy said as she stepped through the window, crunching on broken glass. "They know we're here." She grabbed a backpack from the rack by the door and made her way along the aisles until she found the cleaning products.

Pete waited at the entrance, keeping an eye on Mr Hutson, while Nancy filled the backpack with as many bottles of Mould Blaster as she could find.

She grabbed every bottle from the shelf, threw the bag on her back and turned towards the broken window.

"They're coming," Pete said as he saw a car turning onto the High Street and heading towards them.

No, not a car: a van.

A crowd of Infected appeared from around the corner, following the van. They were moving fast. Running. And now Mr Hutson was coming across the green.

Nancy rushed out of the shop and jumped on her bike, but Pete said, "Wait. I've got a brilliant idea!" and ran inside.

"What are you doing?" Nancy called. "They're coming!"

"Just a minute!" Pete emerged a moment later holding two Aqua-Zap water guns.

"What do you think?" he asked.

"Awesome," Nancy said. "But they'll have to wait!"

Already the van was halfway along the High Street. The Infected were running behind it, spreading out. Nancy could hardly take her eyes off them. She knew them. They were her neighbours and her classmates.

Or they had been.

CHAPTER 11

Screams in the Night

Pete and Nancy pedalled straight past Mr Hutson and into the alley beside the Winchester Arms. They made their way through the village, terrified of being spotted, riding as fast as they could until they came to the gates leading into the Carpenter's Field fracking site.

Pete skidded to a halt and jumped off his bike. Nancy did the same and shrugged off her backpack. Pete ripped the packaging off the two Aqua-Zaps he had taken from Hutson's Hardware. He unscrewed the cap on each gun and held them steady while Nancy poured Mould Blaster into the tanks.

"I've set the nozzle to spray," Pete said as he handed one of the massive water guns to Nancy. They jogged through the gates. "Let's go smother that thing."

"No proble—"

Nancy was cut off by a nerve-shredding *SCREEEEEEEE*. The sound rattled through them like fingernails dragged over splintery wood.

Pete ducked, looking towards the BioMesa building. One of the Infected was standing in the shadows with his head back, his eyes glistening in the moonlight. His mouth was wide open as he screamed.

From the distance came the terrible screeching reply, and Pete knew what it meant.

"They'll be here soon," he said.

CHAPTER 12

The Infected

Pete and Nancy sprinted towards the main building. The Infected man ran at them, moving fast. It was Mr Craven, the Geography teacher from school. Pete had never seen him move so fast. Whatever else the fungus did to people, it definitely made them stronger and fitter.

As Mr Craven came within range, Pete and Nancy raised their water guns and fired. The Mould Blaster sprayed out in a mist in front of them, engulfing their attacker.

Mr Craven stumbled but kept on coming. Pete and Nancy side-stepped to let him past, then turned to watch him lose control of his legs and go down. Mr Craven crashed into the dirt and lay twitching in the mud.

Pete and Nancy didn't stop to see what he did next. They dashed towards the entrance of the main building. But more of the Infected were emerging from the shadows. The air was filled with their screams, and the reply from the crowd behind them was getting closer.

"Quick!" Pete shouted.

Nancy tried to get to the door as Pete fired left and right. He battled to keep the Infected back, but more of them kept coming, blocking the way.

A body hurtled out of the darkness and slammed into Pete. It sent him sprawling. The Aqua-Zap flew from Pete's hands and spun away into the dirt.

Nancy gave up trying to reach the door and turned to raise her water gun, but it

was too late. The Infected were everywhere.
There were too many of them to fight. They
surrounded Nancy from all sides, grabbing her,
overpowering her, forcing her to the ground.

*

The crowd of Infected hauled Pete and Nancy to
their feet. The red van was parked in front of
them.

The Infected were silent now. Waiting.

The van door opened, and Mr Finney climbed
out.

"Dad. Please," Nancy begged as he
approached. "Wake up, Dad. It's me."

Mr Finney was terrifying to look at. His
skin was pale and his eyes were clouded over.
Strands of grey-green fibres covered his lips and
nostrils.

"Come inside," Mr Finney said. "It's time for you to be like us. Soon everyone will be like us." His voice was muffled, as if he was speaking with a mouthful of cotton wool.

The Infected dragged Pete and Nancy into the BioMesa building, where the fungus had erupted from underground. Mr Finney went to one of the strange claws and plucked a pod from its grip. It came away with a soft, wet squelch.

"This is for you," Mr Finney said as he brought it close to the struggling children.

And it burst.

POP!

CHAPTER 13

All Together

Everything happened at once. Pete took a deep breath just before the pod burst, but he didn't have to hold it for long. As the spores filled the air, he heard a metallic bang behind him, followed by someone shouting his name.

"Pete! Nancy!" Krish yelled.

The hands gripping Pete relaxed, just a bit, and he took his chance. Pete pulled away from the Infected, dropped to the ground and rolled. When he jumped up, he turned to see the crowd moving as one, heading for the door where Krish was standing.

"Catch!" Krish shouted.

A moment later, an Aqua-Zap sailed over the crowd.

Pete shifted to a better position as he watched the gun descend. He wasn't the best catcher, and Krish wasn't the best thrower, but it was right on target. All Pete had to do was—

Yes!

As soon as the Aqua-Zap was in his hands, Pete spun around and sprayed the crowd of Infected.

In just a few seconds, they were screaming and writhing in pain.

A light flared close by as Nancy held out her phone torch, aiming it at anyone who came close.

In the bright white light, Pete saw the purple pods shrivel in the mist of Mould Blaster. The claws retracted as if trying to escape its effects. The whole room shifted and squirmed as the fungus reacted.

"The roots!" Krish shouted as he pushed through the crowd towards Pete. "Spray the roots."

They both aimed their water guns at the base of the weird growth and fired.

The Infected and the fungus screamed as one. The twisting sinewy vines withdrew from the ceiling and the walls. They shrivelled and turned grey, breaking into dust like old dry leaves. And in that dust was something that turned Pete's blood to ice. Deep down, close to the hole in the earth, he saw a screaming human face. It was only there for a moment, then it turned to powder and crumbled away as if it had never existed.

All around the building, the Infected collapsed, becoming silent and still. Pete and Krish emptied their water guns at the base of the growth.

"I think that's it," Nancy said as she pointed her torch at the shrivelled mass. "I think it's dead now."

"What about them?" Krish asked, looking at the villagers lying on the floor.

Nancy went to her dad and knelt beside him. She put her hand to the side of his neck. "He's alive," she said as she checked the others. "I think they all are."

CHAPTER 14

Aftermath

The following week, Pete, Krish and Nancy sat on their bikes as they watched what was happening at Carpenter's Field. There were workers everywhere, dismantling the drilling tower and loading containers onto BioMesa trucks. By the end of the day, everything would be gone.

"It'll look like nothing ever happened," Pete said.

"As far as anyone's concerned, not much *did* happen," Krish replied. He had his phone out and was looking at a news article about the events in Crooked Oak last week. "It says no one's sure why everyone woke up at the fracking site. They think maybe it was a mass hallucination caused by contaminated water – chemicals from the fracking process. So BioMesa's closing the site properly now and had to make a big apology. *And* they're going to pay half a million pounds to clean up Carpenter's Field. It'll be ours again."

"So how come none of the Infected remembers?" Nancy asked. "Apart from you?"

"It must be because Pete sprayed me so quickly after I was infected," Krish said. "I can remember the feeling of it taking over my mind, and then I was waking up on the carpet. After that I followed the Infected here and saved your skins."

"What did it feel like?" Pete asked as he watched a van drive up the bank and disappear along the lane. "To be infected?"

"I could feel everyone." Krish took off his glasses. "It was like ... like I couldn't control my thoughts. And I wanted everyone to be like that. I wanted *everyone* to be infected."

"Why?" Nancy asked.

"I don't know." Krish put his glasses back on. "I think the fungus just wanted to survive and spread, like the fungus that takes over ants and makes them explode. Except it didn't make us explode."

"Not straight away," Pete said. "But that face I saw in the earth ... That must have been a person once. Maybe someone from BioMesa. And maybe that's what would've happened to everyone eventually. We would have all turned into one of those things."

"That's why we had to kill it," Krish said.

"There's something I don't understand," Nancy said. "I mean, my mum and dad must've been infected when they came down here to collect those files that night. And then they infected a few people when they took them on that tour of the fracking site a couple of nights later, right?"

"Right."

"So why didn't they infect *me* right away?" Nancy asked.

"I've been thinking about that," Krish said. "And the only thing that makes sense is that the fungus was weaker then. It was still growing, still learning how to control people. They were still your mum and dad ... just a bit ... and they couldn't bring themselves to infect you. But I guess we'll never know for sure – it's a mystery."

"Like on The Mystery Shed," Pete said.

"Well, whatever the reason, it feels good to have them back to normal," Nancy said. She spun her pedals, ready to ride away. "And no more smell."

"You can say that again." Pete smiled. "And now I think I'd like it to stay boring in Crooked Oak. For a little while, anyway."

Our books are tested
for children and young people by
children and young people.

Thanks to everyone who consulted on
a manuscript for their time and effort in
helping us to make our books better
for our readers.